little miss

Scatterbrain

by Roger Hargreaves

© Mrs Roger Hargreaves 1981
Printed and published 1993 under licence from Price Stern Sloan Inc.,
Los Angeles. All rights reserved.
Published in Great Britain by World International Publishing Limited,
An Egmont Company, Egmont House, P.O. Box 111, Great Ducie Street,
Manchester M60 3BL. Printed in Finland. ISBN 0-7498-1554-X
Reprinted 1993
A CIP catalogue record for this book is available from the British Library

Little Miss Scatterbrain was just a little bit forgetful.

You can say that again!

Little Miss Scatterbrain was just a little bit forgetful.

She met Mr Funny.

"Hello Miss Scatterbrain," he said.

"Hello Mr Bump," she replied.

She met Mr Tickle.

"Hello Miss Scatterbrain," he said.

"Hello Mr Strong," she replied.

She met Mr Happy.

"Where are you off to?" he asked her.

She thought.

And thought.

"I bet you've forgotten, haven't you?" laughed
Mr Happy.

Little Miss Scatterbrain looked at him.

"Forgotten what?" she said.

Miss Scatterbrain lived in the middle of a wood.

In Buttercup Cottage.

Everybody knew it was called Buttercup Cottage.

Except the owner.

She kept forgetting.

"I know," she thought to herself. "To help me remember, I'll put up a sign!"

Look what the sign says.

She isn't called little Miss Scatterbrain
for nothing.

Is she?

One winter's morning, she got up and went downstairs to make breakfast.

She shook some cornflakes out of a packet.

But, being such a scatterbrain, she forgot to put a bowl underneath.

"Now, where did I put the milk?" she asked herself.

It took her ten minutes to find it.

In the oven!

After breakfast she set off to town.

Shopping.

She went into the bank first.

"Good morning Miss Scatterbrain," smiled the bank manager.

"What can I do for you?"

Little Miss Scatterbrain looked at him.

"I'd like some..."

"Money?" suggested the bank manager.

"Sausages!" replied Miss Scatterbrain.

"Sausages?" exclaimed the manager. "But this isn't the butcher's. This is the bank!"

"Oh silly me," laughed little Miss Scatterbrain.

"Of course it is. I was forgetting."

She smiled.

"I sometimes do you know."

"Really?" said the bank manager.

"I'd like two please," she said.

"Pounds?" asked the manager.

"Pounds!" agreed little Miss Scatterbrain.

The bank manager passed two pound notes over the counter.

Little Miss Scatterbrain looked at them.

"What are these?" she said.

"Two pounds," he replied.

"Two pounds?" she said.

"They don't look much like two pounds of sausages to me!"

Eventually the bank manager managed to explain, and off went little Miss Scatterbrain, to the butcher.

"Phew!" remarked the bank manager.

Little Miss Scatterbrain walked into the butcher's shop.

"Good morning," said Percy Pork, the butcher.

"Good afternoon Mr Beef," she replied.

"Pork!" said the butcher.

"No!" she said.

"Sausages!"

"But my name isn't 'Sausages'!" he said.

"Of course it isn't," she replied.

"That's what I'm here for!"

"Oh!" said Percy, scratching his head.

"What sort?"

"What do you suggest?" she asked.

"Beef?" he asked.

"I thought you said your name was 'Pork'?" she said.

Percy Pork sighed a deep sigh.

"Call me Percy," he said.

Eventually, after a little more confusion, little Miss Scatterbrain managed to buy her two pounds of beef sausages.

Percy Pork wrapped them up for her.

"Looks like snow," he said conversationally, looking out of his shop window.

"Really?" said little Miss Scatterbrain, looking at the brown paper parcel.

"What a funny man!" she thought to herself.

"Looks like snow indeed! Looks more like wrapped-up sausages to me!"

"Goodbye," said Percy Pork.

"Goodnight," she replied, and went out to catch a bus home.

Little Miss Scatterbrain stood behind Mr Silly in the queue at the bus stop.

Along came Mr Nosey.

He stood behind her in the queue.

He looked up at the sky.

"Looks like snow!" he remarked.

Little Miss Scatterbrain looked at the brown paper parcel in her hand.

And said nothing!